DISNEY'S

My Very First Winnie the Pooh

Growing Up Stories

Stories by **Kathleen W. Zoehfeld**

Illustrated by **Robbin Cuddy**

Introduction by **Tillie Scarritt**

DISNEY PRESS

New York

FIRST EDITION
3 5 7 9 10 8 6 4 2

Library of Congress Catalog Card Number:98-87827

ISBN: 0-7868-3238-X

For more Disney Press fun visit www.DisneyBooks.com

Contents

Introduction • 5

Pooh's First Day of School • 13

Happy New Year, Pooh! • 43

Pooh Plays Doctor • 73

Pooh's Bad Dream • 103

Don't Talk to Strangers, Pooh! • 133

Pooh's Neighborhood • 163

Introduction

The stories in this collection share a common goal: to shed some light on childhood anxieties, and to find ways of empowering children in their wondrous journey of discovery and independence. Even before pre-schoolers venture outside the comforting boundaries of home, they internalize fears, which often take hold of their imaginations. As parents, we try to prepare our children for these new experiences with reassuring words and straightforward answers to their questions.

Children immediately take to Pooh and his friends because they have the same questions, fears, and anxieties as children do. Pooh, being a Bear of Little Brain, is usually the one who poses big questions. And his inseparable friends provide answers from a variety of perspectives.

Generations of children have taken to Pooh and his friends like—pardon the expression—*a bear to honey*, and it is in the Hundred-Acre Wood, this neighborhood of questions, answers, and valuable metaphors, that we present these stories just for preschoolers.

The First Day of School

It is natural for children to resist the idea of leaving the safety of home and going to this

strange place called *school*. As parents, we find ourselves in a hard-sell situation, on the one hand trying to sing the praises of this new experience, while on the other hand remaining an ally and being sympathetic to our child's point of view. We understand that going to school is not only an important and wonderful educational opportunity, but is also a necessary transition toward independence and self-sufficiency. But to a preschool child, it is a scary unknown. In our efforts to demystify the experience, one thing that strikes a chord in children is knowing they are not going it alone. Aside from the fact that their parents will accompany them on this new adventure, children should be reassured that others their age will be there and if they can just be brave and try it, they may even make a new friend.

The words *school* and *teacher* have been echoing in children's heads for weeks, if not months, before the big day arrives. It is probably a good idea not to make too much of it before the first day, to avoid unnecessary anxiety. Reassure your child that you (or their favorite caregiver) will be there at the end of the school day to pick them up. You might want to go and see the school and meet the teacher if possible before the first day. You could even do some dramatic play with your child taking turns to be both teacher and student—a make-believe classroom where some of these fears can air themselves out. Once in school, your child might want a day off to stay at home—affectionately called a "mental health day." Don't be afraid to say yes; your child could be exhausted, could be missing you, or could need a little time to assimilate all the growing he or she has accomplished!

In "Pooh's First Day of School," Christopher Robin, himself a student, puts on the teacher's hat and shows Pooh and his friends that rather than losing their cherished playtime activities, they can have fun at school, *learning fun*. Throughout this story, the use of creative play, as demonstrated in Christopher Robin's play classroom, becomes a wonderful introduction to the world of learning at school.

Welcoming the New Year

At the beginning of life, a child's sense of time is filtered through the period from one nursing to the next, from day to night, from when they last see their parents or caregivers to when they reappear. As children grow, their perception of time matures and is inclusive of full days, weeks, and the calendar days that comprise birthdays and the four seasons of the year. The wonderful regenerative message is knowing that as one day ends, there is always a brand-new one waiting to be born. We all want to create the memories that our children will take with them; and this has to do with allowing periods of reflection on what was, as well as the thrill of what will be.

Keeping a photo album and/or scrapbook with your child is a wonderful way of communicating and instilling this idea of time.

In "Happy New Year, Pooh!" Pooh, Piglet, and Tigger are faced with a sad dilemma: the year has run out of months and there is no way to save it. The great poet Pooh suggests a poem, which he invites his friends to help create. This serves as a means by which all can reflect on the four seasons of the year and the many fun times had by all. Pooh and his friends soon learn that the year is equally filled with the anticipated happy thoughts of what the new year will bring.

Visiting the Doctor

Preparing children for their first visit to the doctor does not need to be a scary experience. Certainly a parent can facilitate a positive experience by researching and choosing the right doctor who best suits their family's needs and style. The doctor's visit can be presented as a shared experience for children and adults alike. We can broaden our children's view on this subject by encouraging them that others are looking out for their well-being in different ways. Doctors and nurses help mom, dads, and caregivers make sure their children are growing well and learning how to stay healthy.

In "Pooh Plays Doctor," children can identify with Pooh as Christopher Robin accompanies him to his first checkup. Rabbit, the nurse, explains to Pooh the use of the doctor's instruments—the reflex hammer, stethoscope, blood pressure armband, tongue depressor, and bandage. This story does not skirt the sensitive issue of getting shots—even though there will probably be a little pain involved, it's nothing a child can't handle. Christopher Robin, the parent in this creative play, understands that it helps Pooh feel safe and secure to know that Christopher Robin will be right there with him every step of the way.

Understanding "Bad Dreams"

Dreams, once recounted, are helpful to parents in understanding what fears or anxieties their children may be feeling. Most often fears in young children pertain to their ever-growing independence and separation from their parents.

Everyday experiences, such as a frightening picture, a movie, a stranger's face, an angry reaction from a parent, sibling, or friend, sleeping alone in a room, or the dark, can trigger anxiety. Confronting a dream head-on may unearth the root of the evil. Parents can suggest a number of ways to empower their children in this regard. Just as mist evaporates on a windowpane, children can be reminded that they have the power to evaporate their dreams with a special word or phrase such as *jelly bean* (whenever "jelly bean" is evoked in the course of a dream, it's "Good-bye, dream"), or a routine that makes the child feel that they are actively doing something to make the bad dream go away or hopefully never happen again. In "Pooh's Bad Dream," children gain the insight that dreams can seem real, but they only happen in your mind. In Pooh's instance, the fear of someone or something stealing his beloved honey is too much to bear. Of course, it's a Heffalump, that elephantine meanie who was only looking for a little companionship in the first place. Nevertheless, Christopher Robin shows his friend that the Heffalump is only made up and that the next time Pooh dreams and meets him, he can just look him in the eye and tell him to go away once and for all. Pooh is empowered by this advice, as children will be when they realize that they are bigger than their dreams and can dispatch any nightmare they choose with a look in the eye.

Learning about Strangers

How do we protect our children from meeting the *wrong* people? None of us wishes to raise our children to be overly sheltered or unfriendly. We would all prefer living in a world where our children can be outgoing and free. However, the reality is we must instruct children that not everyone they meet may be friendly, and since it is difficult to differentiate between a good stranger and a bad stranger, there must be some hard and fast rules to ensure their safety. As a child's world opens beyond the boundaries of his or her home, a whole new set of circumstances arises for both him and his parents. Once again, we are divided in our vision. We want our children to know that this great world welcomes them. There are those whose job it is to protect them and ensure their safety: parents, police, firefighters. There are those, like the mail carrier or doorman of a building, who are doing a job and mean no harm. But just as there are rules in crossing the street, there are rules in dealing with strangers. It is usually a good idea to remind children of these rules whenever they venture out. It is, of course, a bit of a balancing act to warn them and also encourage them.

In "Don't Talk to Strangers, Pooh!" Pooh and Piglet question Christopher Robin about leaving the woods. Christopher Robin explains the Stay-Safe Rules that his mother taught him. These rules are sound advice for parents to share with their children.

Discovering the Neighborhood

One of the great revelations that a child gains in his preschool years is that he or she is part of a larger picture; that this family he thinks everything of is one of many, and that big, wide world out there is ready and waiting to be explored! As they grow, children have an ever-expanding conception of community that includes their families, schools, neighborhoods, cities, countries, and eventually the whole world. "Pooh's Neighborhood" helps

to show that we are infinitely related; our world is made up of people living with and helping other people. Knowing one's environment, one's surroundings, empowers us. Children make mental maps of their little worlds that begin from their bedroom to Mommy and Daddy's room, from the kitchen to the bathroom and that mysterious door that leads out into the world. Understanding our relationship to where we live is a powerful freedom. Here, this concept is explored as Pooh decides to do a neighborly thing and bring a pot of honey to his dear friend Piglet. On his journey to Piglet's house, Pooh has the opportunity to be neighborly to his other neighbors, as well. He helps deliver Rabbit's carrots to Christopher Robin, cheers up Eeyore and, thanks to Owl, gets to see his neighborhood, the Hundred-Acre Wood, from a bird's-eye view. What he sees heartens him, for he realizes that he is a part of a wonderful little world, the world of Pooh and his neighbors.

Pooh's
First Day of School

"School is starting! School is starting!" cried Tigger. "Come on! Don't be late!"

"School?" asked Winnie the Pooh. "What are you talking about?"

"Christopher Robin has a new backpack and lunch box, and he's getting ready for school. We better get ready, too!"

"Oh, Tigger," said Pooh. "School is for children. Not for fluff and stuffing like us."

"What do you mean, not for us?" asked Tigger. "Tiggers LOVE to go to school."

"Piglets don't love school," said Piglet thoughtfully. "At least I don't think we do."

"You're right, Piglet," said Eeyore. "This schooling business—pencils and whatnot—it's overrated if you ask me."

"I think it sounds great!" cried little Roo. "Can I go, too?"

"Come along, Roo," said Pooh. "We'll all go see Christopher Robin. Maybe he can tell us more about it."

Tigger was the first to bound through Christopher Robin's door. "OK, where's the school?" he asked.

"It's about a mile away," said Christopher Robin. "The school bus will come tomorrow morning to take me there."

"A mile?" asked Piglet, pulling his ear.

"It's not here in the Hundred-Acre Wood?" asked Tigger.

"If you have to go that far from home, I'm sure school is not a good thing for Piglets," said Piglet.

"We don't have the brains for it anyway," said Pooh.

"You'd all like school," said Christopher Robin. "I'm sure you would. Wait right here a minute, and I'll make a classroom just for us."

"Imagine, our very own school!" said Pooh. "I wonder if we're up to it."

"Can we bounce in school?" asked Roo.

"Of course you can, little buddy!" said Tigger. "School's the bounciest place there is!"

"There's no bouncing in school," said Eeyore decisively.

"None?" asked Tigger.

"School is work. No time for fun," said Eeyore.

"Not even a little?" asked Tigger. His shoulders drooped.

Eeyore shook his head knowingly.

"Oh," said Tigger, in a very small voice for a Tigger. "Maybe Tiggers don't like school after all."

He and Piglet were about to tiptoe away when Christopher Robin called out, "Time for school to begin!"

"Oh d-dear," said Piglet.

Christopher Robin set up a table, and around it he put chairs, just the right size for Poohs and Piglets.

"We always sing a song first," said Christopher Robin as they gathered around. "*Good morning to Tigger, good morning to Roo. Welcome, all children, good morning to you. . . .* Now everyone join in!"

"This is fun, Piglet. Don't you think?" whispered Pooh.

"Shhh," said Piglet.

"*Good morning*," they all sang.

"If it is a good morning," said Eeyore, "which I doubt."

"Well, the first morning at school can be hard," said Christopher Robin. "But I've met my new teacher, and I know she's really nice. And I know two friends who will be in my class."

"It *is* friendly to spend your days with friends," said Piglet.

"And we learn things in school, too," said Christopher Robin.

"That may be OK for you," said Pooh. "But we're nothing but stuffing. Do you really think a little schooling will improve us?"

"Sure," said Christopher Robin. "You can learn to write your ABCs. It's fun."

Christopher Robin handed out paper and crayons. "Let's all draw pictures of ourselves."

"What does that have to do with ABCs?" asked Tigger.

"The best letters of the alphabet are the letters in our own names," said Christopher Robin. "When our pictures are finished, we can write our names on them."

Pooh chewed the end of his purple crayon. "P-O-O-H," he printed slowly.

"Very nice!" cried Christopher Robin.

"P-T," tried Piglet, whose name was really quite complicated.

Eeyore, who only knew the letter A, wrote "A" under his picture. "Don't know when I've had so much fun," he said proudly.

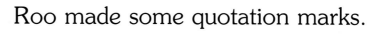

Roo made some quotation marks.
Tigger made a squiggle.
Everyone did a fine job.

"Counting is easy, too," said Christopher Robin. "Pooh, let's see how high you can stack these blocks."

"1, 2, 3, 4, 5, 6," Pooh counted.

It was turning into a lovely tower. But when Tiggers see towers, they think, "Towers are for bouncing," and . . .

CRASH! Down went the blocks.

"Oh," sighed Pooh.

"Tig-ger!" said Christopher Robin sternly.

"Sorry," said Tigger. "All these ABCs and 1-2-3s are fine, but what about fun? What good is a place if you can't even bounce in it?"

"It's true, you can't bounce when your teacher is talking," said Christopher Robin, "but my school has a playground, and we get to go outside and play nearly every day."

"A real playground?" asked Roo.

"Yes," said Christopher Robin. "A real playground with slides and swings and everything."

"I knew Tiggers loved school!" cried Tigger.

But Pooh, whose tummy was beginning to feel a bit rumbly, was worried about something else.

"**I** hope you're allowed to eat at school," he said.

"Oh yes," said Christopher Robin. "That's what my new lunch box is for. I'm going to bring a peanut-butter-and-honey sandwich, a banana, and milk."

"*Mmmm*," sighed Pooh wistfully.

And then Christopher Robin, who knew his friend very well, said, "Why don't we have a little snack right now?"

He set out a large pot of honey, and everyone had a lick.

"Christopher Robin, I hope your new teacher is as nice as you are," said Piglet.

"Yes!" agreed Pooh. "Can we play again tomorrow?"

"PLEASE?!" cried all the rest.

"Of course," said Christopher Robin. "We'll play every day—as soon as I'm home from school."

Happy New Year, Pooh!

"December thirty-first," said Pooh. "Time to turn the page of my calendar." Pooh lifted the December page. "Hmmm." He scratched behind his ear. "No more pages."

"No more months?!" cried Piglet. "That's t-terrible!"

"Oh, Pooh's calendar is just broken," said Tigger. "Let's go look at mine. Tiggers' calendars are never broken."

Tigger bounced into his house and flipped up the December page. He gasped. His tail drooped. "No more months! It's true. What are we going to do?"

"We could make a poem to say good-bye to the months," said Pooh.

"It's too sad," said Piglet. "I can't think of anything to say."

"You can't think a poem, really," said Pooh. "It just has to come to you." He sat down and looked at his paws.

At last he looked up and said: "Good-bye, January, with snow and frost."

"Oh, d-dear," said Piglet, "our whole year is lost!"

"That's good," said Pooh. "It rhymes very nicely."

Pooh continued, "No more February valentine sweets.

"Good-bye, March, with winds and sleets."

"Sleets?" asked Tigger.

"Well, *you* try," said Pooh.

"Tiggers don't do poetry," said Tigger.

"Tiggers can do Tigger poetry," said Pooh.

So Tigger began, "Ahem."

"I'll miss April's drippy rains, and May-sy's crazy daisy chains.

"Did I rhyme it enough?" asked Tigger.

"Yes," said Pooh, "you rhymed enough."

"This is fun," said Tigger.

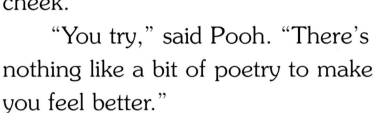

"I'm feeling sadder and sadder," said Piglet. He wiped a tear from his cheek.

"You try," said Pooh. "There's nothing like a bit of poetry to make you feel better."

"I'll miss June," sniffed Piglet, "when the Wood was green, and, *sniff*, all the Julys that might have been."

"Been what?" asked Tigger.

"Well . . . warm and picnicky," said Piglet.

"Mmmm," smiled Tigger.

They sat quietly for a while. Then Pooh brightened.

"I think the rest of the poem has come to me," he said.

Good-bye, August, hot and lazy.

F arewell, September, cool and hazy.

October's colors we'll always remember,
And the pumpkin pies of chill November.

To December, farewell, we'll miss your cheer—

Our favorite month of all the year!

"We don't have to say good-bye to December," said Tigger. "We're stuck here forever."

"Oh, yes," said Pooh. "I forgot."

"F-forever," sighed Piglet.

Toot, toot! Ring a ling ling! Bangety bang!

Piglet, Pooh, and Tigger heard these strange sounds coming from Rabbit's house.

"Maybe Rabbit's in trouble!" cried Tigger. "Let's go!"

Rabbit's house was filled with balloons and colorful streamers.

Toot, toot! Eeyore was trumpeting on a little horn.

Ring a ling ling! Rabbit was ringing a bell.

Bangety bang! Christopher Robin was drumming on a pot with a wooden spoon while Kanga, Roo, and Owl looked on cheerfully.

"**I** wonder why they're so happy," whispered Pooh.

"They haven't heard the sad news," whispered Piglet.

"Well, it's our bounding duty to tell them," said Tigger. He bounced over to Rabbit's calendar and lifted the December page. "I'm sorry to spoil the festivities," he said, "but we seem to have a big problem."

"There will be no more months in the Hundred-Acre Wood," said Pooh.

Piglet wiped another tear.

"Well, I suppose it's to be expected," said Eeyore. "Gaiety, song and dance—it doesn't work for everyone, you know."

"Don't worry, Eeyore," said Christopher Robin, "of course there will be more months."

"There will?" asked Pooh.

Christopher Robin handed Pooh a pot. "Come on! Help us ring in the New Year!" he cried.

"New Year?" asked Pooh. "You mean we have a whole new year ahead of us?"

"Yes," said Christopher Robin.

"With a new January and a new February?" asked Pooh.

"And a whole new March, April, May, June, July, August, September, October, November, *and* December?" cried Tigger.

"Yes," said Christopher Robin. "And look, I've got new calendars for each one of us."

"Wow," said Pooh, "they're beautiful!"

"They're fantabulous!" cried Tigger. "This is so great—we should have a party to celebrate!"

"That's exactly what we're doing," said Rabbit.

 He gave Tigger a horn. "There now—no more moping around! We've got to welcome in the New Year with a HAPPY NOISE!"

Piglet smiled quietly. He thought about the picnics and pumpkin pies he'd be sharing with his friends in the New Year. "It's a very friendly thing to say good-bye to the old year and welcome in the new one with your friends," he said.

"Yes," said Pooh, giving Piglet a little hug. "That's just the way it should be."

Pooh Plays Doctor

"Christopher Robin says it's time for my *animal checkout*," said Winnie the Pooh. "He's bringing his doctor's kit to Owl's house now."

"Doctor's kit!?" cried Piglet. "Oh, p-p-poor P-Pooh, you're sick!"

"Sick!?" asked Pooh. "No—I'm fine. Though I must say I am feeling a bit rumbly in my tumbly."

"That must be it, then!" exclaimed Piglet.

"What's it?" asked Pooh.

"Your tummy—it must be sick," said Piglet.

"Is it?" asked Pooh.

"Isn't it?" asked Piglet.

"Why, yes, it must be. I think," said Pooh. His tummy jiggled and jumped.

"Oh dear," said Piglet. "Let's go together. It's so much more friendly with two."

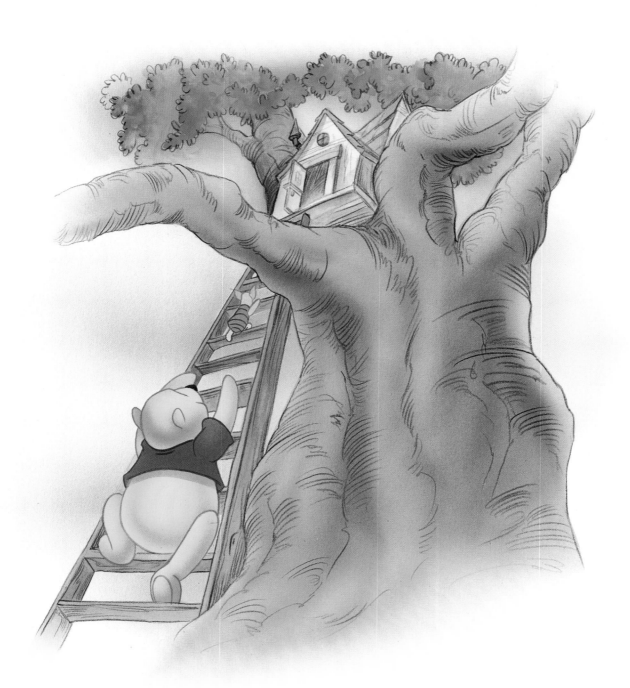

"Step right in, Pooh Bear!" exclaimed Tigger, who had set up a desk near Owl's front door. "It'll be your turn to see Owl just as soon as Roo comes out."

"Christopher Robin, why do I need an *animal checkout*, anyway?" asked Pooh.

"Silly old bear," said Christopher Robin. "Not an *animal checkout*, an *annual checkup*. We need to make sure you are healthy and growing. And this time Owl will give you a special shot to help keep you well."

"A shot!?" asked Pooh. His tummy flopped and flipped.

"A shot!?" piped Piglet. "Oh dear!"

"It's okay," said Christopher Robin. "It will only hurt for a few seconds, and the medicine in the shot will keep you from getting mumps and measles and things like that."

"Bumps and weasels," whispered Pooh to Piglet. "How awful."

"Awfully," said Piglet.

Just then, Roo came bouncing out of Owl's house. "I just had my checkup—it was easy!" he exclaimed. "I'll have a blue one, Tigger, please."

Tigger blew up a nice blue balloon for Roo.

"Come this way, Pooh," said Rabbit, who was being the nurse.

"G-good luck," called Piglet.

Pooh stumped into Owl's house with Christopher Robin right beside him.

Owl's house felt toasty and warm, which was a very good thing, because Rabbit asked Pooh to please take off his shirt.

"Let's sit you up here on the table, my fine young bear," said Rabbit.

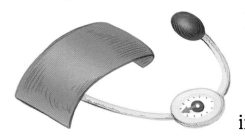

Rabbit wrapped a wide band around Pooh's arm. He pumped air into the band, and it got tighter and tighter.

"How does it feel?" asked Rabbit.

"Tight," said Pooh.

"This gauge tells me your blood pressure is just right," said Rabbit.

"Now step on the scale, and we'll weigh and measure you. . . . Aha! The perfect height for a Pooh Bear of your age, but a bit stout. Still, nothing a little exercise won't cure . . ."

"I do my stoutness exercises every morning," said Pooh.

"Excellent," said Rabbit. "Keep up the good work. If you'll excuse me now, I have a great many important things to tend to. Owl will be right in."

Christopher Robin nodded at Pooh encouragingly, as Owl entered with a flourish. "Well, if it isn't Winnie the Pooh!" he exclaimed. "Splendid day for a checkup, isn't it? I say, how are you feeling?"

"A bit flippy-floppy in my tummy, actually," said Pooh.

"*Hmmm*," said Owl, "let's see." Owl felt Pooh's tummy. He felt around Pooh's neck and under his arms. "Everything seems to be right where it should be."

"Oh . . . good," giggled Pooh.

"Ah, and my otoscope is just where it should be, too—right here in my bag," said Owl.

"An *oh-do-what*?" asked Pooh.

"Nothing more than a little flashlight," said Owl. "And it will help me look in your ears . . . *mm-hmm* . . . your eyes . . . very good . . . your nose . . . excellent . . . and your mouth and throat. Open wide and say *ahhh*."

"*Ahhh*," said Pooh. Owl pressed Pooh's tongue gently with a tongue depressor.

"Wonderful!" exclaimed Owl.

Then Owl pulled a small rubber hammer from his bag. "Reflex-checking time!" he said grandly.

"What's a reflex?" asked Pooh.

"The tiniest tap on the knee, and you shall see," said Owl. Owl tapped Pooh's knee—and his leg gave a little kick.

"Oh, do that again," said Pooh. "That was fun." And Owl did do it again, so Pooh's other leg gave a little kick, too.

"Now, this instrument is called a stethoscope," said Owl. "It's made for listening."

"Listening to what?" asked Pooh.

"Your heartbeat," said Owl. "Would you like to hear?" Pooh listened—*thump-bump, thump-bump, thump-bump*. It reminded him of a poem—a quiet and content poem. And it didn't bother him in the least when Owl said . . .

"Sit right here on Christopher Robin's lap. It is time for your shot."

"I know it will only hurt for a moment, and it will keep me from getting bumps and weasels," said Pooh bravely.

"That's mumps and measles, Pooh," said Owl.

"Could Piglet come in and hold my paw?" asked Pooh.

"Absolutely," said Owl.

When Owl was done, Rabbit popped back in with a bandage. "That'll feel better before you know it," he said, patting 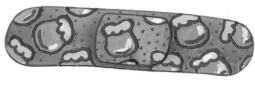 the bandage in place.

"Wow," said Piglet. "You didn't even cry!"

"An annual checkup is no problem for a brave bear like Pooh," said Christopher Robin.

"I'm just that sort of bear," thought Pooh to himself as he wriggled back into his shirt.

"Pooh," said Owl, "you are in tip-top shape, but that stomach of yours is a little rumbly. I prescribe a large pot of honey the moment you get home."

"Christopher Robin," whispered Pooh, "does that mean I can't have any more honey?"

"It means you can have a big pot of it as soon as you like," said Christopher Robin.

"I'd like it soon, then," said Pooh, whose tummy was feeling much, much better.

"T-T-F-N—ta-ta for now!" called Tigger.
"Don't forget your balloon!"

"Thank you, Tigger," said Pooh. And Pooh
let Piglet hold the balloon, as they stumped
home together for lunch.

Pooh's Bad Dream

Winnie the Pooh stood back and admired his work. "Ten new pots of honey," he sighed happily.

"Very nice," said Tigger. "Just make sure that horrible heffalump doesn't eat them tonight."

"The herrable hoffalump!?" asked Pooh.

"He's a greedy gobbler!" said Tigger.

"You've seen him?" asked Pooh.

"No," said Tigger, "but it's even worse when you don't see him. You can't be too careful when a heffalump's sneaking around."

"I'll be careful," said Pooh.

"Worraworrow," growled Tigger bravely. "T-T-F-N—ta-ta for now!"

"Good night, Tigger."

Pooh locked his door. His house seemed big and empty.

He climbed in bed and pulled his quilt up over his nose. And he stayed that way for a long time.

"Hurrible Hoffalump," he thought. "Must keep watch. . . ." He watched and he watched and he watched, until he couldn't keep his eyes open any longer. . . .

Then, suddenly, his house shook like thunder. A big red heffalump crashed through the door. He broke dishes and toppled the lamps. He stomped to Pooh's cupboard and guzzled up three pots of honey.

"Oh!" cried Pooh.

The heffalump turned and looked at Pooh with his horrible green eyes. He snuffled him with his long blue  snout. "Ho-ho!" he said. "Now I'm going to eat you!" The heffalump scrunched a honeypot down over Pooh's head.

"Mmppfh!" cried Pooh.

He jumped out of bed.

He reached up to pull the pot off his head, but . . . the pot was gone! The heffalump was gone, too.

"Where is he hiding?" Pooh wondered. He was afraid to look. He ran to Piglet's house as fast as he could.

"Help! Help! A ho-horrible heffalump is ha-hiding in my huh-house," puffed Pooh.

"A hun? A heff? A who?" asked Piglet, rubbing his eyes.

"A heffalump. Hurry!"

Piglet had no time to think. If he had had time to think, he certainly would not be rushing out in the night to help Pooh find a horrible heffalump.

"Come out, heffalump!" cried Pooh.

Piglet grabbed Pooh's broom and held it high over his head.

"Pooh?" asked Piglet, who had finally had time to think. "What will we do with the heffalump when we find him?"

Pooh thought and thought and thought.

"Maybe we should go get Christopher Robin," suggested Piglet.

"Good thinking," said Pooh.

Christopher Robin was in bed when they arrived. "Poor Pooh," he said, "you must have had a bad dream. Heffalumps aren't real."

"He was real," said Pooh. "I felt him snuffle me with his blue snout. He said he was going to eat me!"

"If there is a heffalump in your house, then Piglet and I will help you find him," said Christopher Robin stoutly.

"We will? I-I mean, yes, we will," said Piglet.

Together they mounted an expedition to find the horrible heffalump and chase him from Pooh's house forever.

They looked under Pooh's bed.

They looked behind his mirror.

They lifted the tablecloth and peered under the table.

They opened his cupboard. All ten pots stood side by side, just as Pooh had left them.

Pooh scratched behind his ear. "It must have been a dream. But why did it seem so real?"

"Dreams can seem real," said Christopher Robin. "But they happen only in your mind."

"Oh," said Pooh, "but if I was asleep, how could my mind be making up a heffalump?"

"Every night, when your body sleeps, your brain stays awake part of the time," said Christopher Robin.

"That's when you're dreaming!" cried Piglet.

"Right!" said Christopher Robin. "Usually dreams are nice—or they're just boring, and you forget them as soon as you wake up. But if you're especially tired or worried about something, then sometimes a dream turns into a bad dream, or nightmare."

"I *was* a little worried," said Pooh, thinking of what Tigger had said. "And I'm so sleepy. But. . . ."

Piglet tucked Pooh in bed.

". . . what if my brain brings the heffalump back?" asked Pooh.

"It's your dream," said Christopher Robin. "You're in charge. If he comes back, just look him in the eye and say: 'Heffalump—go away!'"

"Heffalump go away . . . Heffalump go away . . . Heff . . . go . . . ," Pooh repeated, until at last he was fast asleep again.

Piglet and Christopher Robin tiptoed out.

Then, suddenly, Pooh's house shook like thunder. A big red heffalump stomped right up to Pooh's bed! "Ho-ho!" he boomed.

"Hoffalump, ga-wah . . . H-Hurrfa lumph hahh!" tried Pooh.

The heffalump was muddled. "What?" he asked.

"Go away," said Pooh huskily.

The heffalump stopped. His lip began to tremble. Tears came to his eyes.

"What's wrong?" asked Pooh.

"I just wanted a little snack, that's all," said the heffalump, "and now, *sniff*, you're sending me away?"

Pooh began to feel sorry he had been so rough with the heffalump. "I'm feeling a bit rumbly in my tumbly, too," he said. "Would you like to share a pot of honey?"

The big heffalump looked rather silly sitting in Pooh's little chair. But he didn't seem to mind.

This time, Pooh and the heffalump dreamed a sweet dream together.

Don't Talk to Strangers, Pooh!

One fine day Winnie the Pooh and Piglet were sitting together in their Thoughtful Spot, and when they happened to look up, Christopher Robin was walking down the path.

"Where are you going?" asked Pooh.

"To my grandma's house for supper," said Christopher Robin.

"You're going *out* of the Hundred-Acre Wood, b-by yourself?" asked Piglet.

"My mom and dad say I'm big enough now," said Christopher Robin. "I know I can do it."

Piglet's ears twitched so hard he had to pull on them to make them stop. "Is-is it safe?"

"Sure," said Christopher Robin, "and it feels great to go out on your own sometimes."

"Not scary?" asked Piglet.

"It *was* a little at first," said Christopher Robin. "But my mom wrote down the Stay-Safe Rules for me. Once you know them, being on your own isn't scary at all."

"Can we learn the Stay-Safe Rules?" asked Pooh.

"Maybe *you* can, Pooh," said Piglet, "but it's too hard for a very small animal like me to stay safe."

"You are small," Christopher Robin said, "but you can learn to stay safe, too. The most important thing to remember is—don't ever talk to strangers."

"You mean people who look strange?" asked Pooh.

"Silly old bear," said Christopher Robin, "a stranger is someone you don't know."

"I do know Piglet," said Pooh. "And Piglet knows me."

"Right," said Christopher Robin, "and we all know Tigger, Owl, Rabbit, Gopher, Kanga, and Roo."

"And Eeyore," said Piglet.

"And Eeyore," added Christopher Robin quickly. "They are not strangers."

"Why can't we talk to people we don't know?" asked Piglet. "Are they d-dangerous?"

"Outside the Hundred-Acre Wood there are many, many people," said Christopher Robin.

"Hundreds?" asked Pooh.

"Thousands and thousands," said Christopher Robin. "Most strangers are nice. But a few aren't."

"How can we tell who's not nice?" asked Pooh.

"We can't tell the difference between a good stranger and a bad stranger just by looking," said Christopher Robin, "so we should never talk to any strangers."

"That doesn't sound very friendly," said Pooh.

"You can always be friendly with your friends," said Christopher Robin.

"It's nice to be friendly with friends," smiled Piglet.

"Yes," said Christopher Robin. "But you should never be friendly with strangers."

"Never . . . ," muttered Pooh thoughtfully.

"We can talk more later," said Christopher Robin, hurrying off. "I don't want to be late for supper!"

Well, the word "supper" reminded Pooh that he did not want to be late for *his* supper, either, so he invited Piglet over for honey and haycorns.

Pooh was just beginning his third pot of honey when Piglet looked up suddenly and listened.

"W-what was that?" asked Piglet.

"That's exactly what I was wondering," said Pooh.

"Oh, Pooh," said Piglet, "do you think it's a-a . . . a stranger?"

"It may be," said Pooh. "Sometimes it is, and sometimes it isn't."

*T*ap, *tap*, *tap*, went the noise.

"I think it's someone knocking at the door," said Piglet.

"Is that you, Tigger?" called Pooh. But it wasn't.

"Come in, Rabbit!" he said. But Rabbit didn't.

"What if it's just someone with a little pot of honey for us?" asked Pooh. He started to open the door.

"No!" cried Piglet. "What if it's someone we don't know? Remember what Christopher Robin said."

Piglet pushed a chair over to Pooh's window. He stood on tiptoe and peeked out.

"It's a very strange animal," cried Piglet, "with a shiny yellow head and big round *eyes*!"

Pooh looked, too.

Bang, bang, bang. The strange animal was hammering nails into a small board.

Pooh started to giggle. "He certainly looks strange, but he's not a stranger. That's Gopher. I forgot that I asked him to come over and fix my sign."

"It'ssss all fixsssed," whistled Gopher as Pooh opened the door.

"Thank you, Gopher," said Pooh. "Won't you come in for a cup of tea?"

"I could cccertainly ussse a sssip," said Gopher, pulling off his hard hat and goggles and wiping his brow.

Pooh had just set out the teapot when they  heard another knocking. "Who is it?" called Pooh.

"It's me, Christopher Robin!" called Christopher Robin.

Pooh opened the door.

"Pooh, you really are a very clever bear," said Christopher Robin.

"I am?" asked Pooh. "What did I do?"

"You've learned another of the Stay-Safe Rules all by yourself," said Christopher Robin. "Always make sure you know the person at your door *before* you open it."

"I had a little help from my friend, Piglet," said Pooh. Piglet smiled proudly.

"Grandma gave me a bag of honey cookies to share with my friends," said Christopher Robin.

"Jussst in time for tea," said Gopher.

"Mmmm," said Piglet, "your grandma makes yummy cookies."

"The best in the whole world," said Christopher Robin.

"Can we have more, tomorrow?" munched Pooh.

"Now that you know the Stay-Safe Rules," said Christopher Robin, "you can come along to Grandma's house, and we can ask her together!"

CHRISTOPHER ROBIN'S STAY-SAFE RULES

- Don't talk to strangers.
- Never open your door to a stranger.
- Never take a present from a stranger.
- Never take a ride with a stranger.
- If a stranger does try to talk to you or touch you, yell "NO!," run away, and tell a grown-up you trust as soon as you can.
- And remember, if you're going somewhere, it's always friendlier and *safer* to go with someone you know.

Pooh's Neighborhood

"I say, it's a splendid day in the neighborhood!" said Owl.

"It's a nice day here, too," said Winnie the Pooh.

"Exactly what I'm saying," said Owl, "a perfectly splendid day in the neighborhood."

"Which neighbor wood are we talking about?" asked Pooh.

"Neighbor*hood*," said Owl. "*Our* neighborhood—the place where we live and where all our neighbors live and are neighborly."

"Oh," said Pooh, "it *is* a splendid day in it, isn't it?"

"Quite," said Owl. "Now I'm off for an owl's-eye view!" He flew up and circled once around Pooh's house.

"What does it look like from up there?" called Pooh.

"I can see the Hundred-Acre Wood spread out below me," said Owl. "And it's a fine place, indeed."

As Owl flew off, Pooh began to think about what it means to live in a neighborhood, and he thought perhaps he would bring a neighborly present to his closest neighbor, Piglet.

He took a honeypot out of his cupboard and tied a nice blue ribbon around it.

Then he tucked it comfortably under his arm and stumped down the path toward Piglet's house. But when he reached his Thoughtful Spot, which is halfway between his house and Piglet's, Pooh suddenly had a thought: I *could* take this path straight to Piglet's house. Or—I could go up the path and around the whole neighborhood. And sooner or later the path would take me to Piglet's house, anyway.

And that is what he did.

After he had walked for a time, he came to the house where Kanga and Roo live.

"Hello, Kanga," said Pooh. "I'm just on my way to deliver this neighborly present to Piglet."

"But, Pooh dear, Piglet lives that way," said Kanga, pointing down the very path by which Pooh had come.

"Yes," said Pooh, "but today I'm going the long way."

"Oh, I see," said Kanga. "In that case, perhaps you should join us for a snack."

"Come on, Pooh!" cried Roo. "We're going to the picnic spot."

Pooh said he *was* feeling a bit eleven o'clockish; so they all went together, past the Sandy Pit Where Roo Plays, up to the picnic spot to share a little something.

Half an hour—and one picnic basket—later, Pooh thanked Kanga, tucked Piglet's honeypot back under his arm, and stumped down the path toward Rabbit's house.

"Hello, Rabbit!" called Pooh. "I'm on my way to Piglet's to give him this neighborly present."

"If you're going to Piglet's house, what are you doing here?" asked Rabbit.

"I'm going the long way," said Pooh.

"More like the *wrong* way, if you ask me," said Rabbit. "But since you're here, would you mind taking these carrots to Christopher Robin? I promised he'd have them in time for lunch."

Well, at the mention of the word "lunch," Pooh noticed that his tummy was feeling just the tiniest bit rumbly.

"I'd be happy to," he said.

With carrots under one arm and honeypot under the other, he walked along until he came to the place where the stepping-stones cross the stream.

"One, two, three, four," he counted as he teetered from stone to stone. Eight or nine of Rabbit's friends and relations heard Pooh and peeked out their windows and doors.

Pooh shouted, "Halloo!"

Rabbit's friends and relations waved.

Pooh marched across open slopes of heather and up steep banks of sandstone until at last, tired and hungry, he arrived at Christopher Robin's door.

"Oh, my carrots!" cried Christopher Robin happily. "Thank you for delivering them."

"It seemed the neighborly thing to do," said Pooh proudly.

"Would you like to join me for lunch?" Christopher Robin asked.

And Pooh said, "Well, I really am on my way to Piglet's to bring him this present. But I don't see why I couldn't stop, just for a little while."

After lunch, and a longish snooze, Pooh was back on his way.

He walked down the path through the Little Pine Wood and climbed over the gate into Eeyore's Gloomy Place, which was where Eeyore lived.

"Hello, Eeyore," said Pooh. "I was just on my way to Piglet's house with this neighborly present—"

"Not coming to visit me," said Eeyore. "I didn't think so. It's been such a busy week already. Why, only four days ago Tigger bounced me on his way to the swimming hole. How many visitors can you expect, really?"

And Pooh, feeling rather badly now, offered Eeyore a nice lick of honey.

Pooh opened the jar, and Eeyore peered in. He looked back up at Pooh.

Pooh peered in. "Empty," he said.

"That's what it looked like to me," said Eeyore.

"Oh bother," said Pooh.

He stumped off glumly, trying to think how he was going to tell Piglet about the neighborly present Piglet was not going to get.

Pooh had almost arrived at the Place Where the Woozle Wasn't and was deciding to take the long path around it, just in case the woozle was, when he saw Owl flying over.

"I've seen our whole neighborhood today," Pooh told him. "But now I have no neighborly present left for Piglet."

"The bees have been quite busy at the old bee tree lately," said Owl. "Perhaps you can get a fill-up there."

"That's a good idea, Owl, but it's such a long way," sighed Pooh.

"Come along," said Owl. "We'll take the shortcut through the woods."

So they walked together until they came to an open place in the middle of the forest, and in the middle of this place was the old bee tree. Pooh could hear a loud buzzing near the top.

Up, up, up he climbed.

"Go up higher!" called Owl. "Past the bees. To the very top of the tree. Now, look all around you. What do you see?"

The Hundred-Acre Wood was spread out below him.

"Our neighborhood!" cried Pooh. "Our beautiful home!"

"That's the owl's-eye view," said Owl grandly.

"Oh, I can see poor Piglet out sweeping his walk," said Pooh. "Looks like he could use some company."

Nice Place for Picnics

Sandy Pit Where Roo Plays

Pooh's House

POOH'S THOTFUL SPOT

Piglet's House

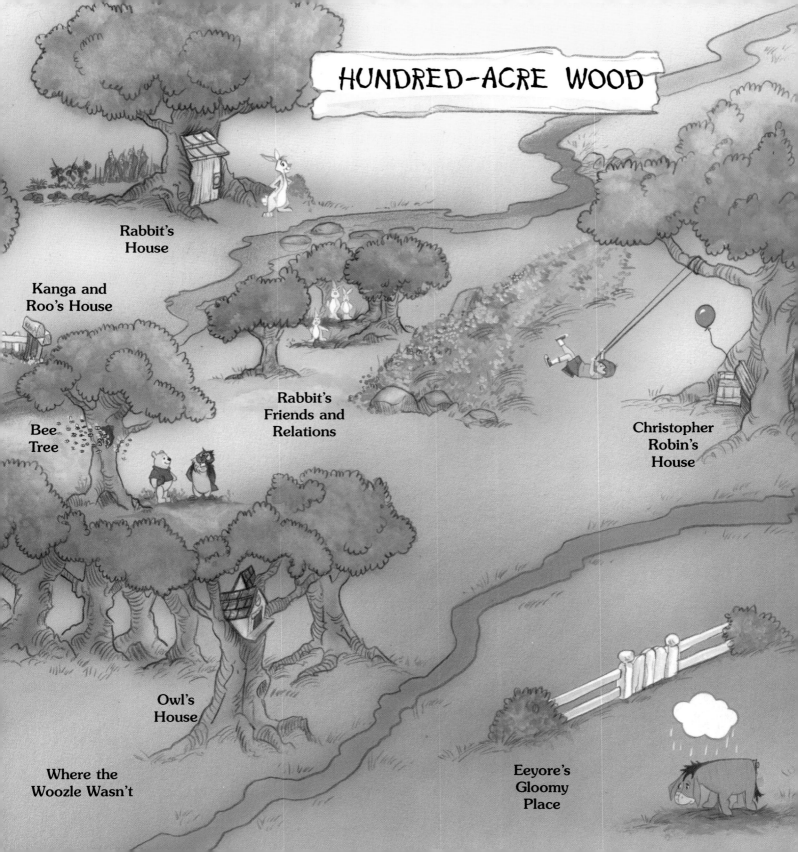

HUNDRED-ACRE WOOD

Rabbit's House

Kanga and Roo's House

Bee Tree

Rabbit's Friends and Relations

Christopher Robin's House

Owl's House

Where the Woozle Wasn't

Eeyore's Gloomy Place

So Pooh filled the honeypot once more, and he and Owl went to Piglet's house for supper.